Prologue

Hidden behind some rocks, Spirit, a magnificent dolphin with striking yellow markings, lazily watched the younger dolphins searching the seabed for a strand of seaweed. His wife, Star, was watching them too.

"I've found some," clicked Bubbles, digging in the sand with his nose and uncovering a long, green, crinkly piece.

"Good," clicked Swift, an athletic dolphin with a sleek, muscular body. "Now we can play seaweed tag. Who wants to be 'it'?"

"Me," squeaked Velvet, shyly swimming forward.

As she reached out to take the seaweed from Bubbles, Swift swam in front of her, blocking the way.

"Who said you could play?" he clicked bossily.

"N-n-no one," said Velvet uncertainly. "But I can, can't I?"

"No," Swift clicked. "Boys only. Go away."

Star went to intervene, but Spirit stopped her.

"Wait a moment," he said softly. "Let's see if they can sort this out for themselves."

Just then Bubbles swam forward and tossed the seaweed down in the sand. "If Velvet can't play then I don't want to either," he said.

"Boys only," said Swift firmly. "And you *will* play or else."

As he spoke, Swift seemed to grow larger. The other young dolphins huddled together, nervously watching what would happen next.

"Or else what?" asked Bubbles calmly. "You don't scare me. Come on, Velvet. Let's go play somewhere else."

Swift stared in surprise as Bubbles and Velvet left with the other dolphins chasing after them calling, "Wait for us. Can we play too?"

When they'd gone, Star smiled at Spirit.

"Bubbles did well," she said. "It takes courage to stand up to someone who looks stronger than you."

"He did," clicked Spirit proudly.

"The Silver Dolphins do well too," Star mused. "They stand up for us and our oceans."

"The Silver Dolphins are very brave," Spirit agreed. "We are lucky to have them."

Chapter One

ntonia Lee and Sophie Hastings were on their way to school.

"Antonia, were you listening to anything I've been saying?" asked Sophie, gently tapping her best friend.

Smiling apologetically, Antonia took Sophie's arm and linked it with hers.

"Sorry, Soph. I was, but then I got distracted by that seagull cawing. It reminded me how much there is to do at Sea Watch right now."

Sophie sighed and rolled her eyes, but she was only joking.

"Forget Sea Watch for just one minute," she said. "This is exciting news. You know that TV programme *Stage Struck*? The one about the teenagers who go to a drama school? Well, it's coming here, to Sandy Bay, to film for the new series!"

"You don't watch *Stage Struck*," said Antonia, waving at Cai and Toby who were waiting at the school gates.

"Not very often," Sophie agreed, "but it's still exciting. There are lots of opportunities for artists on a film set: scenery, make-up, costumes, that sort of thing. I'm definitely

going to go and watch the filming. I might learn something new."

Sophie was mad about art and rarely went anywhere without her sketch book and a pencil.

"The film cast and crew are arriving today. Dad says everyone's staying at the Sandy Bay Hotel. They've taken over two whole floors and the penthouse suite."

"Not you as well!" exclaimed Toby. "Everyone's talking about *Stage Stuck*."

"*Stage Struck*," Sophie corrected him.

Toby gave her a cheeky grin and, realising he was teasing her, Sophie groaned.

The whole school was buzzing with the news and soon Antonia was fed up of hearing about *Stage Struck*.

"Not long now," whispered Cai, as they filed into afternoon assembly.

Antonia glanced at the clock. Fifteen minutes until the end of the school day, then she and Cai would be free to go to Sea Watch, the marine conservation charity run by Cai's great-aunt Claudia. She could hardly wait! She didn't hear a word that the headmaster, Mr Cordier, said. Antonia rested her hand lightly on her school polo shirt, knowing that her silver dolphin charm necklace was hidden underneath it. Jewellery was forbidden at Sandy Bay Primary School, but Antonia never went anywhere without her special necklace.

Antonia and Cai shared a wonderful secret. They were Silver Dolphins, guardians of the sea. When the dolphins called to them through their special jewellery, Silver Dolphin magic allowed Antonia and Cai to swim with real dolphins so they could look after the ocean

and the creatures living there. Silver Dolphins were rare. Claudia was a Silver Dolphin too, although she rarely answered the call these days.

"Antonia Lee, I said Year Six could lead out," said Mr Cordier. "It's home time."

Antonia's face flamed red as the rest of the school giggled.

"She wasn't listening because she's thinking about *Stage Struck*!" hissed Lauren nastily.

"She's not such a big fan as you are!" Becky whispered loyally.

"I know," Lauren's voice became louder as they moved out of the hall and filed along the corridor back to class. "I've got all the old series on DVD. I've got posters round my room and the fact-file diary. And soon I'm going to have autographs of the whole cast. Mum

bought me an autograph book to collect them in. What do you think of that, Toni?"

"That's nice," said Antonia.

Lauren eyed her suspiciously. "I suppose you'll get an autograph book now!"

Antonia ignored her and concentrated on getting her things ready to go home. When the school bell rang she stood smartly at her desk with her bag packed and her fleece on.

"Antonia, Alicia, Sophie, Charlie, Cai and Toby can all go," said Mrs Howard.

"Hmmph!" grumbled Lauren as Antonia walked past her. "I bet I get their autographs before you do."

"What was all that about?" asked Cai, as they set out to Sea Watch together.

Antonia shrugged. "Lauren seems to think I'm dying to meet the cast of *Stage Struck*."

Cai laughed. "Like you've got time for that!"

When they arrived at Sea Watch, Claudia was pleased to see them.

"Someone's just brought in a razorbill with oil on his feathers. I'm about to start cleaning him up, so if you could feed the herring gulls and clean out their cage and see to Tilly that would be very helpful."

Antonia's heart skipped a beat.

"Has there been another oil spill?" she asked.

"No, this bird's just been unlucky enough to find a patch of oily sea. Boats often leak small amounts of oil."

Sighing softly, Claudia went to fetch an apron and some thick gloves.

Antonia and Cai took a quick look at the razorbill before starting their jobs. "He looks very fed up," commented Antonia.

"I'm not surprised," said Cai. "Look at the state of him."

Razorbills in the wild were proud-looking birds, black with snowy-white chests and a distinctive white line on their beaks. This bird's feathers were clogged with oil and his white parts were a grimy grey.

"Steady," soothed Antonia, as the bird let out a frightened growl.

The bird stared at her and after a bit gradually relaxed.

"It's amazing how you do that," said Cai.

Before Antonia could think of a modest reply, Claudia returned with a solution to cleanse the bird's stomach of poisonous oil and a special washing-up liquid for his feathers.

"Let's get started," she said, putting the solutions next to the sink.

Antonia and Cai put on gloves and aprons and went outside.

"Who shall we do first?" asked Cai.

"The gulls," answered Antonia, wanting to save her favourite animal until last. Tilly the seal had been at Sea Watch for many months now, much longer than expected, but after several setbacks she was finally fit enough to return to the sea. Antonia was pleased that Tilly was going home, but she was really going to miss her.

There were four gulls in the outside aviary; two with broken wings, one with a broken leg and the other with injuries to her chest. Like most of the herring gulls around Sandy Bay, they were an inquisitive bunch who stared unnervingly at Antonia and Cai while they worked.

"They're so greedy," said Cai. "They're only watching us to see if we've got something to eat."

"I know," said Antonia. "The other day that big one nearly pecked off my finger thinking my cleaning cloth was food."

When the aviary was clean they left the birds squabbling over a bucket of fish and went to feed Tilly, who was in the deepwater pool.

The friendly seal swam over, sticking her whiskery nose out of the water and honking a hello.

"Hello, Tilly," said Antonia, careful not to touch her.

The animals at Sea Watch weren't pets and for their own safety it wasn't good for them to become too familiar with people.

Tilly swam around the pool grunting noisily as Cai and Antonia brushed and hosed down the walkway. Next they fed Tilly, throwing fish into the water to make her swim for her dinner.

"That was fun," said Antonia, as they returned to the Sea Watch building.

Inside, Claudia was rubbing the razorbill dry with an old towel.

"It's very quiet today. Where is everyone?" Antonia asked, suddenly missing her friends from the secondary school.

"They're not coming. Emily texted to say everyone's gone to wait for the cast of some TV show to arrive," said Claudia.

"Huh!" snorted Cai. "I thought they had more sense than that."

Claudia smiled. "It's OK. Everyone works so hard for Sea Watch. It's not fair to expect

volunteers to come every day. Emily said they'd be here tomorrow. Are you all right, Antonia? You seem troubled."

Antonia and Claudia were very good at knowing what each other was thinking. A bad feeling had suddenly come over Antonia, but she wasn't sure why. Shaking the feeling away, she said brightly, "I'm fine. I can stay a bit later tonight, so what shall I do next?"

Chapter Two

Antonia was starving when she got home. It was meatballs in tomato sauce for tea. She tucked in hungrily, spearing a meatball with her fork and popping it in her mouth as the phone rang.

"It's Sophie," said her mum, passing the telephone over.

Swallowing quickly, Antonia took it.

"Hi, Sophie, what's up?" she asked.

Sophie was breathless with excitement. "The film crew are shooting their first scene in Sandy Bay early tomorrow morning. Mum says I can go and watch for a bit before school. Do you want to come with me?" she asked.

It sounded fun, but Antonia had already promised to meet up with Cai.

"Sorry, Sophie, but we've some last-minute things to do before the launch of the Litter Fishing scheme. Remember I told you about it – giving free rubbish sacks to fishermen? Sea Watch is co-ordinating it for Sandy Bay."

"Never mind," said Sophie cheerfully. "I'm taking my sketch book so I probably won't be great company anyway. See you at school."

"Have fun," said Antonia, putting the phone down.

The following morning as Antonia put her lunchbox into her school bag, a familiar and exciting sensation came over her. The dolphins were going to call! Thank goodness she was walking to school alone. Antonia hurriedly pulled on her shoes and fleece, and said goodbye to Mum and little sister, Jessica.

"Bye," called Jess, as Antonia rushed out of the front door.

Suddenly the dolphin charm hanging around Antonia's neck began to vibrate. Seconds later a shrill whistle sounded.

Silver Dolphin, we need you.

Spirit, I hear your call, Antonia answered in her head.

Antonia ran, following the Coastal Path until

it forked, then taking the right-hand lane that led down to Gull Bay. The dolphin charm beat out a rhythm on her neck. Antonia loved the feel of its silky-soft tail thrumming against her skin, urging her to hurry. She ran on, past the tiny beach shop, shuttered now but due to open at the start of the holiday season in a few weeks' time. At last she arrived at Gull Bay.

She pulled off her shoes and socks and left them with her bag at the top of the beach. The powdery sand felt cold and crunchy under her feet as she ran for the sea.

"Eeek!" The water was freezing and numbed her feet and legs.

Ignoring the discomfort, Antonia splashed through the surf until the icy water reached her thighs. Taking a deep breath, she lunged

forward and swam. A few seconds later her legs melded together, flicking at the sea like a tail. Excitement fizzled through her. The water didn't feel at all cold now. Expertly, Antonia used her hands like flippers and, arching her body, leapt in and out of the water as gracefully as a dolphin.

Spirit, I'm on my way, she whistled.

The thrill of becoming a Silver Dolphin was something Antonia knew she'd never tire of. Using Spirit's vibrations to guide her, she swam underwater to him. She didn't have to travel far. Spirit and his family were waiting a little way round from the headland. Seeing Cai approaching from the other direction Antonia swam faster, reaching the dolphins first and shooting him a playful smile.

"You came quickly, Silver Dolphin," said

Spirit, rubbing his nose against Antonia's in greeting.

Spirit was a proud-looking animal with intelligent eyes, a silver head and a striking yellow blaze that ran along his side from his face to his dorsal fin.

Cai swam up, and as he greeted Spirit, Antonia said hello to Star, Dream and Bubbles.

"Flipper Feet," squeaked Bubbles, splashing her in a friendly way.

"Today it's a litter-picking task," said Spirit. "There's a lot of rubbish in the sea by the cliffs."

"Can we help the Silver Dolphins, Dad?" Bubbles asked.

"Yes, but be careful. Don't touch anything sharp and keep away from plastic bags."

"Bubbly!" clicked Bubbles. "Race you to the cliffs, Silver Dolphins."

Without waiting for an answer, Bubbles swam away, his body flashing silver as he dived in and out of the water.

Antonia, Cai and Dream gave chase, but Bubbles won, reaching the cliffs before them by several tail-lengths.

"Yuk!" said Antonia, suddenly noticing the floating rubbish.

There was a plastic drink bottle, two empty crisp packets, a chocolate bar wrapper, an empty sandwich container and a train timetable that was soggier than old cornflakes.

"City people," said Antonia, squinting at the timetable. "These times are for underground trains."

Cai was from the city, but was living with his Aunty Claudia while his parents worked abroad in Australia.

"Country people are just as bad for littering," he said defensively.

"I know," said Antonia. "What I meant was that this rubbish comes from visitors and not from local people."

Fishing the chocolate bar wrapper and timetable out of the water, she stuffed them into one of the crisp packets.

Cai emptied a strand of seaweed out of the sandwich carton and tucked the rest of the litter inside it.

"Is that all?" he asked, looking around.

"I found something," said Dream, nosing a polystyrene coffee cup towards him.

"Thanks." Cai scrunched up the cup to make it fit inside the sandwich carton. "Let's get this ashore and find a bin."

"Bubbly!" clicked Bubbles, somersaulting.

"That was quick work. Now we can play."

"Not today," Antonia said, pulling a sad face. "We have to go to school."

Bubbles smacked the sea with his tail.

"You're always going to school!" he said disgustedly.

Antonia and Cai laughed. "It feels like it," they agreed.

"Can't we have one quick game of sprat?" asked Bubbles, his dark eyes pleading.

"Bubbles, I'm sorry, but we have to go. Mum works at our school so I can't be late or I'll be in trouble with her too."

"Next time," clicked Cai. "We'll play sprat and seaweed tag."

"OK then," Bubbles agreed.

Bubbles and Dream swam with the Silver Dolphins back to where they'd first met.

"My shoes and bag are at Sandy Bay. I'll wait for you there," said Cai.

Antonia shook her head. "You'd better not. I think I can get to school on time from Gull Bay, but there's no point in making us both late," she said.

"Bye, Bubbles, bye, Dream."

Clutching the rubbish, Antonia struck out for Gull Bay. There wasn't a second to lose. If Antonia wasn't in school before Mrs Howard called the register, she'd have to sign in at the office where her mum worked as a receptionist. Then there'd be trouble. Mum would want to know why, having left the house before Jessica and her, Antonia had managed to arrive after them. With determined strokes, Antonia swam on.

Chapter Three

When Antonia finally arrived at school, hot and out of breath, the playground was deserted. She hurried indoors, hung up her fleece in the cloakroom and went straight into the classroom. The class watched in silence as she came through the door. Warm with embarrassment, Antonia sat down.

"Sorry I'm late," she mumbled.

"You're just in time," said Mrs Howard. "I'm about to call the register. I suppose you've been watching the filming too?"

"No, I…" Antonia hesitated. She didn't like telling lies, but she couldn't tell Mrs Howard where she'd been.

Luckily for her the door opened and Charlie came in late too. With an exaggerated sigh, Mrs Howard stood up and lectured the whole class on how lateness would not be tolerated and how they were not to let the excitement of having a film crew around stand in the way of their education. At playtime Lauren grabbed Antonia by the arm as she came out of the girls' toilets.

"So what happened to you this morning?" she asked, pushing her large face into Antonia's.

Shaking her arm free, Antonia carried on walking.

"Where were you?" Lauren persisted, following her. "You were watching the filming, weren't you? That's why you were late."

"None of your business," Antonia answered, heading for Sophie, Cai and Toby who were standing in a group on the opposite side of the playground.

"I bet you didn't get any autographs. The director said the actors were too busy to sign autographs until lunchtime."

Antonia stopped walking and swung round to face Lauren, her green-grey eyes holding Lauren's small, hazel ones.

"Not that it's any of your business, but I was nowhere near the film crew this morning," she said firmly and, giving Lauren

a pitying look, Antonia moved on.

"Loser," Lauren bellowed after her. "I'm a much bigger fan of *Stage Struck* than you. I know everything about the actors. I even know where they're filming next and I'm not telling you!"

Cai ran over to Antonia. "Are you all right?" he asked.

Antonia grinned. "I'm used to it," she said. "She doesn't scare me."

Antonia happily forgot all about Lauren and *Stage Struck* until after school, when she was back at Sea Watch. Emily, Eleanor and Karen were there too, chattering away together.

"*Stage Struck* is filming in Gull Bay tomorrow," said Emily, colouring in a poster for the Litter Fishing launch. "*Danny Appleton* told me when he came into our shop to buy

a present for his little sister. He's my favourite actor. He's so cool. I wish I had an older brother like Danny."

"Me too!" Eleanor and Karen agreed.

Hiding their groans, Antonia and Cai escaped outside to clean Tilly's pen and feed her.

Tilly was pleased to see them, as always. Honking noisily, she climbed out of the deepwater pool to see what Antonia was doing with the mop.

"Aunty Claudia says we'll let her go after the Litter Fishing launch," said Cai.

"Shoo." Antonia gently shook the mop at the grey seal. "I hope she'll be all right. She's too nosy for her own good sometimes."

"She'll be fine," said Cai reassuringly. "There are a couple of friendly seals that hang around

the harbour. The fishermen throw them fish to eat."

"The fishermen round here are really nice," said Antonia, propping the mop against the mesh fencing and unreeling the hose. "It's great that they've agreed to take part in the Litter Fishing project."

"They like fishing in clean seas," said Cai. "Some of the stuff that comes up in their nets is horrible."

"I know," Antonia shuddered, thinking of the nasty things she'd seen in the ocean. "I'm glad Sea Watch is co-ordinating the project. I can't wait for the launch. It was nice of Claudia to ask us to give the fishermen their new sacks."

"Do you think the scheme will put the Silver Dolphins out of a job?" joked Cai.

"Never," said Antonia, hosing his feet.

"You rat!" Cai lunged for the hose, but Antonia darted out of his reach.

The Litter Fishing project had been arranged by an environmental organisation. They were providing free sacks for fishermen to put rubbish caught in their nets in, rather than throwing it back into the sea. The sacks could later be emptied into a special container at the harbour. Claudia had agreed that Sea Watch would keep a supply of the sacks and arrange for the container to be emptied when full.

"Turn the hose off, Antonia. I'm going to get Tilly her food."

Tilly enjoyed swimming after the fish that Antonia and Cai threw for her. Gracefully, she zipped round the pool, diving deep then surfacing in a completely different place.

"She's a great swimmer," said Cai when the bucket was empty. "Not long now, Tilly. Soon you'll have the whole sea to play in."

"I hope she finds some friends to play with," said Antonia.

"She will," said Cai. "Stop worrying about her. She's going to be fine."

On her way home from Sea Watch, Antonia was so busy thinking about Tilly that she didn't see Lauren and Becky coming up the path until she'd practically walked into them.

"Where do you think you're going?" snapped Lauren crossly.

"Sorry, I didn't see you there," said Antonia, misunderstanding Lauren and sidestepping her to walk on.

"If you're thinking of hanging around the

film crew, you're too late. They've packed up for the day," Lauren called after her.

Antonia kept walking.

"Huh! Think you can ignore me, do you? Well, you'll be sorry tomorrow when everyone hears my news."

Antonia didn't know what Lauren was talking about until the following day, when Lauren smugly announced to the whole class that she and Becky had been hired by the director of *Stage Struck* as extras.

"Anyone would think she'd got the lead role," grumbled Sophie, at home time, "but it's not even a speaking part. Extras are just there in the background. You don't even notice them."

"Just ignore her," said Antonia. "She's so

wrapped up in being a film star that she hasn't been nasty to anyone all day."

"That's true," said Sophie, brightening. "What are you doing after school?"

"I'm going to the Litter Fishing launch with Claudia and Cai. Why don't you come along too? It'll be fun."

"Thanks, but it's not my kind of thing. Come round some other time then?"

"Definitely," said Antonia. "I'd like that."

Chapter Four

The moment school ended Antonia and Cai raced to Sea Watch. Claudia was still tending to the oiled razorbill, who'd needed a second bath.

"Can you put him back in his pen for me while I go and tidy myself up?" she asked.

While Claudia went to put on clean clothes

and comb her unruly hair, Antonia and Cai donned thick gloves and carried the razorbill to the back room.

"He looks so much better than when he first came in," said Cai.

"He's not as nervous either," said Antonia, gently putting the bird down in his pen. They topped up his water, then went into the house to wait for Claudia.

"Wow!" exclaimed Cai when Claudia finally appeared in the kitchen dressed in a smart skirt with a matching jacket. "Who are you? You're not my aunty."

"You look lovely," said Antonia.

Claudia blushed. "I thought I'd better make an effort," she said. "Lots of important people will be there, and at the reception afterwards."

The launch was being held at the harbour,

so there was no point in taking the car. On the walk there they stopped several times to admire the posters made by Sea Watch volunteers to advertise the Litter Fishing scheme. The harbour was packed with fishermen and sightseers, and Antonia got an attack of the butterflies as Claudia steered her to the front of the crowd where a small stage had been erected. When Claudia had asked if she and Cai wanted to present the fishermen with their litter sacks, Antonia hadn't realised that she'd be doing it in front of an audience.

As she climbed on to the stage, Antonia noticed her mum and Jess amongst the crowd. Jess's face lit up when she saw Antonia and she waved excitedly. Antonia waved back, then Jess waved with both with hands, nudging Mum and making her wave too.

"Aw, sweet," said Cai, blowing Jess a kiss.

Antonia felt a sudden rush of pride for her little sister. Jess was an unbelievable pain at times, but she could be lovely too. Seeing her cheering them on calmed Antonia's nerves.

The presentation ceremony started with Claudia giving a short talk to explain how the Litter Fishing scheme worked and how it benefited everyone. A local politician had been invited to speak too, but unfortunately he gave a much longer talk. Antonia stifled a yawn. She was bored of standing still for so long and was beginning to get fidgety. She glanced at Cai and grinned. He was bored too, if his fixed smile was anything to go by. It looked like it had been painted across his face. A funny feeling came over Antonia and she inwardly groaned. Spirit was about to call.

Now what? The politician was still talking so she and Cai couldn't just leave – they hadn't yet presented the sacks to the fishermen. Panic-stricken, she glanced at Claudia.

The dolphins need us, Antonia said, inside her head.

I know, Claudia answered silently.

Claudia took a step forward and when the politician paused for a breath she smoothly interrupted. "Thank you, Mr Fielder. And now the moment I know you've all been waiting for. If our two representatives from the fishing community could come forward, Sea Watch will present them with their new litter sacks."

The politician shot Claudia a startled look as Antonia and Cai hastily handed over their yellow sacks and shook hands with two burly fishermen. Someone in the crowd cheered and

everyone started clapping. Antonia felt her silver dolphin charm leap to life. As its tail beat against her skin an accompanying whistle shrilled through the air. Even though only a Silver Dolphin could hear the whistling cry, Antonia was still grateful that everyone was busy clapping. She and Cai walked quickly from the stage and disappeared into the crowd, worming their way between people until they were free.

"Shame about missing the reception," said Cai, running alongside Antonia. "There was going to be a buffet."

Antonia laughed. Trust Cai to think of the food. She was just grateful that Claudia had helped them to get away. Unsurprisingly, on a chilly March afternoon, the beach was deserted. Antonia and Cai ran to the rocks

where they pulled off their shoes, socks and fleeces. They hobbled across the sharp stones and splashed into the sea.

Silver Dolphin, we need you.

"Spirit, I hear your call," Cai called as he walked further out.

Antonia waded alongside him until together they dived into the water, gasping as the coldness hit them. But the moment she started swimming, Antonia forgot about the cold. Her legs melded quickly and kicking them like a tail she swam, arching her body in and out of the waves.

"This way," called Cai, swimming eastwards.

"We're being called towards Gull Bay," said Antonia, swimming alongside him.

Just before they rounded the cliff, Antonia

saw a silver head in the water. Spirit had come alone and there was clearly no time for a greeting.

"A bird is suffering. Follow me," he clicked.

Diving deep into the sea, Spirit swam fast, slicing through the water until he was round the headland. Antonia and Cai followed behind Spirit in silence until he suddenly pointed his nose upwards and surfaced near an outcrop of jagged rock. Antonia and Cai broke through the water on either side of him – Antonia pushing her long, blonde hair out of her eyes and Cai coughing up a mouthful of water.

"Up there," clicked Spirit, tossing his head in the direction of the rocky cliff.

At first Antonia couldn't see anything. She screwed up her eyes, scanning the rocks until at last she saw a bird on a bumpy ledge. It

was hopping round in frightened circles while frantically flapping its wings. From its short, black legs Antonia thought it was a kittiwake, but she couldn't be sure because the poor bird's head was engulfed in plastic. Its claws sounded like rain tapping on the ledge as it struggled to get free. Antonia swam closer and, gripping the rocks with both hands, pulled herself out of the water. Barnacles scrapped at her knees and feet making her eyes sting, but Antonia carried on climbing until the bird was only a head-length above her. Sensing her presence, it panicked, warning her off with a shrill cry.

"Steady there," called Antonia. "We're here to help you."

"Antonia," hissed Cai.

Antonia didn't hear him. She was too busy

watching the bird frantically hopping backwards. What if it fell off the ledge?

"Hush," she whispered. "Stand still. We won't hurt you."

The bird stood rigid, its grey body trembling. Antonia was dimly aware of a buzzing noise coming from her left, but ignoring it she reached out to pull herself up to the bird's level.

"Antonia!" Cai's shout was low and urgent, and it stopped Antonia from going any further.

She turned her head and stared out to sea in disbelief. Cai and Spirit had vanished. Only a rippled patch in the water showed where they'd been. A small motorboat was speeding towards her. Where had that come from? She had thought Gull Bay was empty when they'd arrived, but maybe it wasn't. In the distance,

Antonia could see a cluster of people moving around on the sand. The boat's engine tone changed from an angry buzz to a quiet hum as it approached the rocks. Neither of the two passengers, a middle-aged man and a young woman wearing smart clothes and lots of make-up, looked happy.

"You there," shouted the man, pointing straight at Antonia. "What the blazes do you think you're doing?"

Chapter Five

The man's angry voice made Antonia feel wobbly inside. Clutching at the rocks for support, she wondered how to explain what she was doing, without giving away the secret of the Silver Dolphins. Then the kittiwake made another desperate attempt to free himself from the plastic.

"Steady there," said Antonia, reaching up to him.

"Did you hear me? We're trying to film here and you're spoiling our sightlines."

Something snapped inside Antonia and she glared down at the man.

"I'm helping this bird," she said icily. "It's going to suffocate."

As she spoke Antonia could feel the magic draining out of her in a tingling stream. No! This couldn't be happening. Not now, when the kittiwake was in so much danger. But it was too late. Sadly Antonia realised that the people in the boat had broken the magic.

Spirit, she called silently.

Silver Dolphin, don't... Antonia could hardly hear Spirit's reply. She closed her eyes blotting

out everything around her, but it was no good. His voice had faded away.

Impulsively, Antonia tried to grab the plastic from round the kittiwake's neck. She moved too fast, startling the bird and he flapped his feathers and lashed out, almost scratching her with a black claw.

"Get in the boat!" shouted the man. "We're taking you back to the beach."

"It's for your own safety," the lady added, in a gentler voice. "We can't leave you here on the cliff."

Antonia hardly heard them. She stared at her hands. She should have taken things more slowly. It was obvious that the poor bird was petrified.

"What about the bird? We can't leave him. He'll die."

"It's a seagull," said the man harshly. "No one will miss it."

Antonia knew that kittiwakes were a special type of gull, but she was too outraged to correct him. He might be able to leave an animal to die, but she couldn't. Furiously, she tried to pull herself on to the kittiwake's ledge, but the rocks were harder and much more slippery than when she'd climbed up using her Silver Dolphin magic. Realising that it wasn't safe to carry on, Antonia finally admitted defeat. Swallowing her disappointment, she climbed down and meekly allowed the lady to help her into the boat.

"How did you get here?" asked the lady, as Antonia sat down. "Did you climb round the cliff?"

Antonia hesitated. Thankfully the magic had

mostly dried her clothes, so they were just a little damp in places and it didn't look like she had swum there.

"I climbed over the rocks," she said.

"Didn't you see us filming?" snapped the man, not looking at her, but keeping his eyes fixed on the shore.

"I didn't realise," Antonia stammered. "Aren't you filming on the beach?"

"We are mostly, but we could see you in some of the long distance shots," said the lady gently. "I'm Louise, by the way, assistant film director. And this is Mr Harry Brewer, our director. Are you a fan of *Stage Struck*?"

Antonia shook her head. "I don't watch much television," she said.

"Too busy rescuing seagulls," said Mr Brewer, with a false laugh.

Antonia was shocked by Mr Brewer's attitude. She was also cross with herself for getting caught. It had been careless. She might have blown the secret of the Silver Dolphins. Thank goodness Cai had been smarter than her. Maybe he could rescue the kittiwake. Hope sparked in Antonia's eyes. Yes, of course he would. And she could help him by distracting attention away from the cliffs.

"So, um, how long are you going to be filming in Gull Bay?" she asked, resisting the urge to look for Cai and Spirit.

When the boat was in shallow water Mr Brewer cut the engine. He wore sandals with no socks and rolled up his trousers before climbing out.

"You're one crazy girl," he said to Antonia,

as he indicated for her to get out too. "Do you always go around in bare feet?"

"My shoes are over there," she replied, waving vaguely at the beach.

"Well, do me a favour. Put them on and go home."

He raised his voice for the benefit of the crew, cast and spectators watching with interest. "Crazy girl!"

Antonia glared at the back of Mr Brewer's head. There were plenty of rude things she could say about him right now, but none of them would help the kittiwake. In a dignified silence she walked round the crowd of smirking onlookers until she was finally off the beach. Several times she thought she heard her name being called, but Antonia refused to look back. She was sure that plenty of people

58

from school had witnessed her humiliation. No doubt they'd all be talking about it tomorrow. She focused on the edge of the beach and kept walking up the steps, on to the hard ground and along the lane until she reached the shuttered beach shop. Then she stopped. Now what? She couldn't go home without her shoes again. There would be too many questions from Mum. Claudia had bailed her out when she'd got stuck without shoes in the past, but she was at the launch party for the Litter Fishing scheme. Antonia couldn't interrupt that either.

Of course you can!

Claudia's voice sounded so clearly in her head it was as if she was standing beside her.

I'm always here for you, Silver Dolphin.

Claudia! Antonia felt tears of relief welling

at the corners of her eyes and she swallowed them back.

I'm at Gull Bay.

I'll be with you shortly, Claudia answered.

While Antonia waited she wondered where Cai was. She was hopeful that he would have rescued the kittiwake and be on his way home by now. Would he be cross with her for getting caught? Antonia felt hot then cold with shame. Maybe it was a good thing she'd almost been discovered. It would certainly remind her to be more careful in future. Reaching inside her school polo shirt, she lifted the dolphin charm out and held it in her hand. The dolphin's body was warm and silky-soft to touch. Did she deserve the trust of the Silver Dolphins?

Spirit, I'm sorry.

The dolphin's tail flicked lightly against her skin. Antonia smiled. She might feel bad about what had happened, but Spirit had already forgiven her. Hearing a car in the lane, she tucked the charm back inside her clothes and smoothed down her hair. Seconds later the car appeared with Claudia in the driver's seat, looking uncharacteristically smart in her suit, and Cai next to her, smiling and waving. The remaining guilt lodged inside Antonia evaporated. Cai had forgiven her too. Everything was going to be fine.

Chapter Six

"I rescued the bird," said Cai proudly, twisting round in his seat. "He was a bit dazed, but he wasn't injured."

"Well done. I can't believe I was stupid enough to get caught," said Antonia. "I didn't even hear the boat."

She quickly explained what had happened

to her after she'd been plucked from the cliffs, ending her story with an apology.

"Don't worry about it," said Claudia. "We all make mistakes. You didn't give away any secrets and you're safe, and that's the main thing."

"It won't happen again," Antonia vowed. "I'm going to have eyes everywhere."

"I rescued these too," said Cai, passing Antonia's shoes back to her. "It was a tough job. The pong nearly knocked me out."

"Ha ha! Thanks, Cai." Gratefully, Antonia shoved her feet into them.

"And guess what?" Cai paused dramatically. "The bag the bird got stuck in must have been dropped by the film crew. It had 'short microphone' printed on the side."

"That's terrible!" Antonia exclaimed.

"I'm going to have a word with the film crew tomorrow," said Claudia. "They probably don't realise how dangerous litter can be."

She turned the car into Antonia's road and stopped outside her house.

"Your bag is at Sea Watch, but Cai can give it to you at school. It's Friday tomorrow, so would you like to stay the night, Antonia? I'm releasing Tilly this weekend. We could do it early Saturday morning before anyone's about."

Antonia's stomach turned a somersault. It was exciting that Tilly was finally going back to the sea, but she was still only a little seal.

"Yes, please, I'd love to stay," Antonia said. "And thanks again for the lift."

"You're welcome," said Claudia.

Antonia didn't feel like going indoors straight

away. She went through the side gate and stood in the back garden, staring out at the sea. It was like looking up into space. The ocean stretched away from her – an enormous expanse of blue, full of hidden mysteries and dangers. Soon Tilly would be out there and they'd probably never see her again. Antonia shivered apprehensively then quickly scolded herself. She was being silly. The sea was where Tilly belonged.

"Antonia, you're home!"

Jessica hurtled into the garden and threw herself at her big sister. "You've been ages. Was the Litter Fishing party good? It was so exciting seeing you and Cai up on that stage. Were you nervous?"

"Slow down, Jess," said Antonia, laughing. "Let's go inside and I'll tell you all about it."

* * *

When Antonia walked into the classroom the following day, Lauren leapt up and clapped loudly.

"Here she is, let's hear it for the crazy girl!" she jeered.

"Yay! Crazy girl!" shouted Becky, enthusiastically clapping along.

"What are you like?" Lauren sounded friendly, but her eyes were spiteful. "Mr Brewer, our director, said he's had all sorts of problems with fans, but he's never met anyone quite as crazy as you. What did you think you were doing?"

"I was rescuing a bird," said Antonia coldly. "It had a plastic bag wrapped round its head." She nearly added that the bag had been dropped by one of the film crew, but changed her mind. Lauren would probably accuse her of making that up.

"Loser," said Lauren.

"No, you're the loser," said Sophie, jabbing her finger at Lauren. "Leave her alone."

Antonia's tongue was jumping with retorts, but she held them back, knowing it would only encourage Lauren. Touching Sophie on the arm she said quietly, "Thanks, but let's just ignore her. She's not worth it."

Sophie glared at Lauren, then deliberately turning her back on her said, "Antonia Lee, you are too nice. And you're definitely not a loser."

It was one of the longest Fridays ever. At every opportunity Lauren kept whispering, "Crazy girl," and "Loser," at Antonia.

"She doesn't frighten me. If she did then I'd say something to Mrs Howard," Antonia said sensibly to her friends.

When the bell went at 3.15pm, Antonia and Cai were some of the first out of school. They hurried to Sea Watch, stopping off at the house to put Antonia's overnight bag indoors. As they came down the garden towards the Sea Watch building they could hear Claudia and Sally, an adult helper, calling out loudly to each other.

"What's going on?" asked Cai, breaking into a run.

"It's Tilly," said Antonia.

Tilly the seal wriggled round the Sea Watch building and, catching sight of Antonia and Cai, honked excitedly at them. She was being pursued by Claudia and Sally, both puffing hard even though Tilly wasn't moving very fast. Antonia and Cai ran towards them so that Tilly was surrounded. Realising she

couldn't go anywhere, Tilly uttered a playful grunt and smacked her tail on the ground.

"She's like a puppy," said Cai, "I keep thinking she's going to roll over and beg for her tummy to be scratched."

"She would if we encouraged her," said Antonia. "She's too friendly for her own good."

"And nosy," said Claudia. "Sally accidentally left the gate open and Tilly was through it in a flash. The sooner she gets back to the sea the better. She's bored here."

Together they herded Tilly back to the deepwater pool. It was a slow job as Tilly awkwardly wiggled her way across the grass, but once she was back in the pool she moved like an arrow, swiftly speeding through the water.

Claudia closed the gate to the deepwater

pool and then locked it. "Right," she said. "I'm going along to Gull Bay to have a word with the film crew."

Antonia froze, hoping Claudia wasn't going to ask them to go with her. She could just imagine what Lauren would have to say about that on Monday.

"Sally, are you all right to stay and keep an eye on things for me while I'm gone? Great, thanks. And you two," Claudia nodded at Antonia and Cai, "please could you dig out the large cage so we can transport Tilly to the beach? We'll need to drive her to a spot further down the coast tomorrow. If we let her out on our beach she might decide to stay."

Antonia huffed out a sigh of relief. "No problem. Shall we clean out the gulls too?"

"Emily, Eleanor and Karen asked if they

could do the gulls today. But you could clean out the razorbill. He's looking much better now that he's had a second bath."

While Antonia and Cai cleaned out the razorbill's cage they argued about what to call him.

"Billy," said Cai firmly. "Billy the razorbill."

"Billy's too similar to Tilly," said Antonia.

"Tilly won't be here after tomorrow," said Cai. "What? Don't look at me like that. I'm going to miss her too, but this bird definitely looks like a Billy."

"Urr," said the razorbill, as if he was agreeing with him. "Urr, arrc, arrc."

Antonia and Cai fell about laughing.

"You win," said Antonia, giggling. "Billy he is."

Once the razorbill was in a clean cage with

fresh water and some fish for tea, Antonia and Cai went to look in the shed for the large cage. It didn't take long to find. When the shed was erected, shortly after the deepwater pool had been built, Claudia decided that keeping it tidy could be one of the volunteers' chores.

"There's no point in storing things in a shed if it's too messy to find them again," she'd said.

They left the cage by the deepwater pool, said goodbye to Sally who had a couple of little jobs left to do, then walked up to the house.

"That's good timing," said Cai. "Here's Aunty Claudia."

"She doesn't look happy," said Antonia, quickening her step. "I hope everything's OK."

Claudia parked the car in the driveway and climbed out, raising her eyebrows at Antonia and Cai.

"That did not go well," she said crisply. "Mr Brewer was most unhelpful. He said he had more important things to worry about than litter. When I pointed out that not only could it kill the local wildlife, but it also ruined the scenery, he said that he paid people to work for him and if I wanted the countryside cleaned then perhaps I should do the same!"

"He really said that?" Cai was aghast.

"He did," said Claudia, forcefully shutting the car door. "The assistant director looked pretty shocked too. It's a shame she's not in charge. The only thing we can do now is to have a litter pick every evening once the film crew has packed up."

"We'll help," said Antonia and Cai at once.

"Thanks," said Claudia. "We'll start today after tea. They'll have finished filming by then. If you two could get some disposable gloves and bags ready, then I'll start cooking."

"I don't like Mr Brewer," said Antonia, heading towards the Sea Watch building. "He's rude and inconsiderate."

"At least he doesn't live here," said Cai thankfully. "I wonder what's for tea. I'm starving."

Chapter Seven

The following morning Antonia, Cai and Claudia put Tilly in the cage, loaded it into the back of Claudia's car and drove her to a secluded beach several miles west of Sandy Bay. The tide was out and it was a long walk down to the sea. Tilly was heavy and halfway there they stopped for

a rest, gently placing the cage on the sand. Antonia shoved her hands in her pockets to warm them up. There was a cold sting to the March air and she was glad it was Tilly and not her who was about to go into the water.

"Ready?" asked Claudia.

Antonia and Cai nodded, then took up their positions on opposite sides of the cage.

"Not far now," Claudia reassured them as they lifted Tilly again.

The sand became darker and more compact, glistening with water and strands of seaweed that squelched under Antonia's feet.

"Here," said Claudia, stopping about a metre from a line of surf licking at the sand.

Carefully, they lowered the cage down with its door pointing seawards. Tilly's whiskers

twitched excitedly and she rattled the cage door with her nose.

"Impatient!" said Antonia, chuckling.

"It's probably best if one of us opens the door and everyone else waits further up the beach so Tilly isn't distracted," said Claudia. "Who wants to let her out?"

"You do it," said Cai to Antonia.

Antonia smiled gratefully. Cai knew she had a huge soft spot for Tilly.

"Bye, Tilly. Have fun and be good," he said.

Claudia walked round the cage studying Tilly as if she'd never seen her before.

"She's fine," she said at last. "Definitely ready to go home. We'll wait up there for you Antonia, by the boulders."

Claudia set off with Cai scurrying alongside her. Antonia waited until she and Tilly were

alone. To her surprise, her heart was hammering like a drum. She took a deep breath to calm herself before unlocking the cage door.

"Bye, Tilly. Be safe."

The impatient seal nudged the door open and, grunting happily, wriggled on to the sand. She lifted her dappled-grey head and sniffed the air then, without so much as a backwards glance, headed into the surf. Antonia bit the inside of her cheek, determined that she wasn't going to cry. This was the best result ever. They'd nursed Tilly to good health without making her tame or dependent on people.

She kept her eyes on the seal as she splashed happily into the water and swam away. Picking up the cage, Antonia hurried up the beach to Claudia and Cai.

"Another Sea Watch success," she said, forcing a smile.

They stood and watched Tilly's shiny head bobbing in the sea until the seal dived underwater and was gone for good.

Antonia didn't say much on the way home, but once she was back at Sea Watch there was so much to do she stopped worrying and immersed herself in the chores. The rest of the weekend flew past. On Sunday morning she caught up with Sophie, who had tons of new sketches and gossip about the film set to share.

"The actors are really nice," said Sophie excitedly. "Danny Appleton signed my sketch book and Kate Mellor, who plays Ellie, gave me a jar of body glitter. Kate's sister is an artist and she uses body glitter like paint. Kate said I should try it too."

On Sunday afternoon Antonia reluctantly did her homework. She had twice as much now she was in Year Six and it seemed twice as difficult too! Then it was all the usual Sunday evening chores – washing her hair, checking her school bag and helping Mum make up the lunchboxes ready for the following day.

By Monday afternoon the weekend was a distant memory and Antonia felt like she'd been back at school for days.

"I can't wait for home time," she moaned to Sophie as they worked together on a model of a glacier for their geography project.

"There's only an hour to go," soothed Sophie. "Are you going to Sea Watch or do you want to come to Gull Bay with me to watch the filming?"

"Thanks for the offer, but I'm going to Sea Watch," said Antonia.

However, when Mrs Howard asked the class to clear up at home time, Antonia knew that Sea Watch would have to wait. Sensing that Spirit was about to call, she cleared up in record time, stuffing her pencil case and empty lunchbox into her bag just as her silver dolphin charm leapt to life. At the first flick of its tail, Antonia glanced over at Cai. He nodded, showing he'd felt it too, and rapidly piled his possessions into his bag. The bell sounded, but Antonia hardly heard it. Her attention was on the shrill whistle that only she and Cai could hear.

Silver Dolphin, we need you.

Spirit, I hear your call, she silently answered.

Antonia stood by her chair, anxious that

Mrs Howard would notice she was ready and let her go. Every second of delay in the classroom could make a difference if Spirit's call was urgent. Gradually the class quietened. Mrs Howard scanned the room.

"Well, that makes a nice change," she said, smiling straight at Lauren Hampton. "Lauren, Becky, Antonia and Cai, you were ready first so you can all go."

Faster than athletes starting a sprint race, Lauren and Becky grabbed their bags and made for the door. Spurred on by the dolphin charm thrumming against her neck, Antonia beat them to it.

"Out of the way!" shrieked Lauren. She barged past, knocking Antonia against the door frame and almost pushing her flat on her face.

Gulping back the pain, Antonia regained her balance only to be shoved again by Becky.

"Lauren, Becky, come back here at once," thundered Mrs Howard. "I can't believe what I'm seeing. I didn't let you go first to attack other members of the class. Apologise to Antonia at once."

"I'm fine, really," said Antonia, keen to be on her way.

"This is not fine. I will not tolerate such loutish behaviour. Lauren, Becky, I'm waiting for you to apologise."

The look Lauren gave Antonia was pure poison and made her toes curl. It was all very well Mrs Howard insisting on an apology, but Antonia knew she would pay for it later and also it was holding her up. Luckily Cai knew better than to wait. After checking that Antonia

wasn't hurt, he slipped past her to answer Spirit's call.

"Sorry." Lauren and Becky finally spat an apology at Antonia.

Tossing her head, Lauren turned to Mrs Howard, "We have to go, Miss, or we're going to be late. Becky and I have parts in *Stage Struck*."

Mrs Howard sighed. "Go on then. And no running in the corridor," she shouted after them.

Antonia's dolphin charm was beating urgently against her neck. Slinging her bag back over her shoulder, she hurried along the corridor at a fast walk. Thank goodness the call had come now, not later when she would already be home. It would be easy to slip into the water unseen at Sandy Bay, whereas it

would have been impossible nearer her house at Gull Bay with the film crew there. Once outside, Antonia broke into a run, weaving her way round the parents, grandparents and children congregating on the playground. There was no sign of Cai. Glad that he was already on his way, Antonia raced through the school gates and headed for the sea.

Chapter Eight

When she reached the rocks at Sandy Bay, their favourite place for going into the water, Antonia found Cai's bag and shoes stacked in a neat pile. Adding her own things to the mound, Antonia clambered over the rocks and stepped into the water. It was freezing cold, but she forced herself to go

deeper, clenching her chattering teeth together until the sea came up to her thighs. Then taking a deep breath, she plunged in head first. Seconds later her legs melded together and she forgot about the cold. This was the best feeling ever. Using her hands like flippers and kicking her tail-like legs, Antonia swam northwards out of the bay to Spirit and Cai.

She caught Cai up in the open water and swam alongside him, arching her body above the waves in time with his.

"That was quick," clicked Cai.

They swam on until Antonia saw four silver heads bobbing in the water. "Over there," she clicked, swimming towards them.

"Silver Dolphins, thank you for answering my call," whistled Spirit, as they approached. Quickly he rubbed noses in greeting, but there

was no time to say hello to Star, Bubbles and Dream.

"This way, Silver Dolphins," instructed Spirit. "An animal is stuck in a crab pot."

Antonia was mystified. Why had Spirit called them to free an animal from a crab pot? It didn't sound like the kind of task that the Silver Dolphins usually undertook. If the creature wasn't a crab, then the fisherman would release it when he checked his pots. She glanced at Cai, but he shrugged his shoulders then dived after Spirit.

They swam in a procession, Spirit leading followed by Antonia and Cai, with Star, Bubbles and Dream bringing up the rear. Spirit took them over a kelp bed and its dark-green fronds reminded Antonia of a forest. A school of fish flittered past, their bodies flashing as

they sped through the green water. As they approached some rocks, Spirit slowed and Antonia glanced around in surprise. Why were they stopping here? There were no crab pots, only an ancient-looking basket nestled against a rock.

"That's it," said Spirit, halting.

Antonia looked at the basket again and realised it *was* a crab pot. A very old one draped with seaweed and covered with barnacles. She swam closer.

"Careful, Silver Dolphin," clicked Bubbles.

Antonia stared at the pot. Something was jammed inside it, but she couldn't work out what. She swam round to the other side and, looking into the basket, swallowed a scream. Pressed against the mesh a large, human-like eye stared back at her. The skin around the eye was baggy and orange as if the creature was very old. Antonia felt her skin coming out in goose bumps as the animal shifted and pressed a suckered arm against the cage.

"It's an octopus," breathed Cai.

Antonia's stomach looped the loop.

"An octopus!" she exclaimed. "But we don't get octopuses round here."

"Try telling him that," said Cai, leaning closer. "Isn't he amazing!"

"Careful," warned Antonia. She knew it was illogical to be scared. Octopuses were shy creatures that kept out of the way unless attacked, and this one was trapped. But there was something about its saggy body and long tentacles that revolted her.

"We have to let him out or he'll die," said Cai, examining the crab pot for a catch. "This

cage must have been lost or forgotten. Stray crab pots are becoming quite a problem round here. Aunty Claudia's hoping the new Litter Fishing scheme will clear some of them up. Forgotten cages are called ghost pots and if an animal gets stuck inside one it eventually dies of starvation. Then its body becomes bait for another animal and so the cycle starts again."

Cai found the catch and went to release it, but Antonia cried out in alarm, "Wait! We can't just let it out. Octopuses don't naturally live round here. The water's too cold. What if it's injured or sick? It's impossible to tell with it all squashed up like that."

"Good point," said Cai thoughtfully. "So what shall we do?"

Antonia shifted slightly so that the octopus

no longer seemed to be staring right at her. "We could tow the crab pot ashore," she said hesitantly, "and take him to Sea Watch."

"That wouldn't work," said Cai. "He needs to be in water. Anyway, how do you think we're going to carry an octopus to Sea Watch unnoticed? It's not like walking a stray dog there."

Antonia giggled nervously, then said, "How about we tow it to the shallows and one of us looks after it while the other goes to Sea Watch for Claudia. I don't mind going," she added hurriedly.

"Or you could ask Claudia to come to us," said Cai, giving her a meaningful look.

"Yes, I suppose I could," said Antonia quietly.

"Can we go with the Silver Dolphins?" asked Bubbles suddenly. "Please, Dad?"

Spirit smiled indulgently. "Yes, you can. Be careful though. Don't swim too close to the shore."

"Bubbly! Thanks, Dad." Bubbles turned a somersault in the water.

Bubbles and Dream positioned themselves at the back of the crab pot leaving Antonia and Cai at the sides. It was easy to move the cage with so many of them pushing it. Antonia kept her fingers on the cage's frame to avoid touching the octopus, but the animal barely moved. If anything it seemed to make itself smaller. Antonia smiled at her silly behaviour. What had she expected? That the octopus would try to escape and engulf her in its suckered tentacles like a monster from a science-fiction film?

As they swam into Sandy Bay, Dream clicked

for everyone to stop. "We better not go any further," she said sensibly.

Bubbles said goodbye to Antonia, then dived under the crab pot to say goodbye to Cai. Dream said a quieter goodbye, then side by side the dolphins swam back out to sea.

The cage was more awkward to move with only Antonia and Cai pushing it. When they reached shallow water they stood up and walked with the cage until the water lapped around their ankles. Sea water poured from their clothes, leaving them completely dry. Antonia shook her slightly damp hair back over her shoulder.

"Is here OK?" asked Cai, stopping.

"It should be," said Antonia. "There's an incoming tide so we might have to move the cage again if it gets too deep."

Cai fell silent as Antonia stared at the horizon.

Claudia.

She imagined Claudia working away at Sea Watch, maybe cleaning out Billy the razorbill's cage or entering data on the computer.

Silver Dolphin, is something wrong?

It never failed to amaze Antonia how quickly Claudia responded. It was as if Claudia already knew she needed help.

We've found an octopus, thought Antonia, trying to keep the fear and revulsion out of her head. But she couldn't fool Claudia, and hearing her low chuckle brought a smile to Antonia's face.

An octopus! I'll be right there.

Sighing with relief, Antonia said to Cai, "Claudia will be here soon."

"Good," said Cai vaguely.

He walked round the crab pot studying every centimetre of the octopus's squashed orange body.

"Come round here," he said, excitedly flapping his hand. "You can get a really good look at his suckers. They're awesome. Did you know octopuses are very clever? They can find their way through mazes, open boxes and even unscrew jars."

"That's nice," said Antonia. Crossing her fingers, she really hoped that the octopus didn't decide to demonstrate its box-opening talents before Claudia arrived.

Chapter Nine

As Antonia and Cai waited for Claudia, a lady out walking her dog on the beach came over to see what they were doing. She was amazed to see the octopus and even Antonia became slightly more enthusiastic about their exotic find. After taking some photos on her mobile phone the woman carried on up the beach.

News of the octopus spread fast and lots of passers-by stopped to have a look at it. Antonia was grateful when Claudia arrived and took control of the situation, asking the people to stand back and give the octopus some room.

"Are we taking him back to Sea Watch?" asked Cai.

"No. We don't have facilities for warm-water animals so I've called the local aquarium," Claudia answered. "It looks like this could be them now."

But the man, who was carrying a camera, and the lady striding purposefully towards them were from the *Sandy Bay Times*.

"What luck!" said the photographer. "We were covering another story when we heard there was an octopus on the beach."

He took lots of pictures of Antonia and Cai with the octopus, while the journalist asked how they'd found it.

"The crab pot came in with the tide," said Cai, his cheeks turning darker with the fib. "We waded out and pulled it in, then phoned my Aunty Claudia for help."

The photographer left after he'd finished taking pictures, but the journalist hung around waiting for the aquarium staff. Finally two men dressed in jeans and T-shirts bearing the aquarium's red logo arrived. They were carrying a small tank which they put down on the sand.

"Hi, I'm Will and this is Tim," said the fair-haired man.

"Claudia Neale, from Sea Watch, and my volunteers, Antonia and Cai," said Claudia, shaking hands.

Then Will crouched down to examine the crab pot. "Looks like a Common Octopus," he said. "They're normally found in much warmer seas such as the Mediterranean, but we've had a few sightings of them around the English Coast recently. It's because the sea's getting warmer. This is the first time one's been caught. These ghost crab pots are a real danger to sea life."

"A ghost crab pot, what's that?" asked the journalist eagerly.

"A crab pot that's been abandoned or lost," said Cai and Antonia together.

"You know your stuff then," said Tim approvingly. "If you ever lose interest in Sea Watch, give us a call. We'd give you both jobs at the aquarium!"

"Thanks," said Antonia and Cai, laughing.

"We'll take this beauty back with us," said Will. "We can assess it properly at the aquarium and then, depending on its health, we'll either arrange for it to go somewhere warmer or keep it in captivity."

"Will you give it a name?" the journalist asked.

Tim looked at Antonia and Cai. "Any ideas?" he said.

"Legs," said Antonia with a shudder, making everyone laugh.

Will and Tim filled their empty tank with sea water, then very carefully transferred the octopus into it. Before they put the lid on, Antonia and Cai had a good look. Legs was even bigger than Antonia had imagined now that he had room to spread. He was almost a metre in length from the top of his soft, rounded

body to the tip of his muscular, orange tentacles. It was his eyes that gave Antonia the creeps. They were too human for comfort.

"Come and visit him," said Will. "We'll tell the receptionist to let you in for free."

"Thanks," said Cai. "That sounds great."

When the beach had cleared, Antonia and Cai rescued their things from the rocks and sat on the promenade to put on their socks and shoes.

"Never a dull moment," commented Claudia. "Gull Bay needs clearing up next. Do you want to help or have you had enough for one day?"

"Will the camera crew have gone home?" asked Antonia, not wanting to run into the nasty director again, or Lauren and Becky for that matter.

"They've moved into town temporarily," said

Claudia. "They were setting up as I came through to find you."

"I'll come then," Antonia volunteered. "It'll be easier to clean up now than if the rubbish ends up in the sea and Spirit has to call us to collect it."

"I'll come too," said Cai. "But what happens if we get another call to go to Gull Bay whilst they're back filming *Stage Struck* there?"

"You'll manage," said Claudia confidently. "You're Silver Dolphins."

The rest of the week followed a pattern, with Antonia and Cai starting off at Sea Watch and finishing at Gull Bay to clear up after the film crew. Antonia was amazed and disgusted at the amount of litter they left behind. It was doubly annoying since the local fishermen

were doing such a good job with the Litter Fishing scheme. In less than a week, the container in the harbour was almost full.

Once or twice Antonia and Cai had seen Lauren and Becky leaving the beach with the actors from *Stage Struck*. Lauren always put on a silly, loud voice making sure Antonia noticed her. At school she continued to taunt Antonia, calling her "Crazy Girl" and "Saddo".

"She's always hanging around on the beach trying to meet the cast," she told everyone.

Antonia laughed it off with Cai, Sophie and Toby, but deep down she was getting fed up with Lauren.

On Thursday morning, Mrs Howard arrived with a newspaper and waved it excitedly at the class. "Incredible news," she said, beaming at everyone. "We have two celebrities amongst

us. It's all here in the *Sandy Bay Times*. Does anyone know who our new celebrities are?"

Lauren practically fell off her chair. She ran a hand through her short, brown hair and proudly stuck out her chest. "It's me and Becky," she said, lowering her head in an attempt to seem modest. "As most of you already know…"

Rustling the newspaper, Mrs Howard held it up for the class to see.

"Sorry to interrupt, Lauren, but it's Antonia and Cai," she announced proudly. "I had the surprise of my life seeing your faces smiling out at me over my cereal this morning. What's this I've been reading about you rescuing an octopus from certain death?"

Before Antonia could speak, Lauren leapt out of her seat and snatched at the

newspaper. "You've got the wrong page," she snapped.

Mrs Howard held the newspaper out of reach. "Sit down, Lauren," she said sternly.

"But there's an article about me in there. A journalist came and interviewed Becky and me when we were filming. She's not a celebrity," said Lauren, jabbing a finger at Antonia. "I am."

A few of the class began to giggle, but Mrs Howard silenced them with one of her looks.

"We will look for your article in a minute," she said crisply. "First, Antonia and Cai, come up here and tell us your story. It sounds fascinating."

Chapter Ten

A ntonia and Cai explained how they'd rescued the octopus and Mrs Howard searched for a picture of one on the Internet, displaying it on the white board.

"You rescued that!" exclaimed Isabel, in awe. "I would have been too scared to go anywhere near it."

"I was a bit scared," said Antonia honestly. "But octopuses don't usually attack people and this one was trapped in the crab pot."

"It was still a brave and smart thing to do," said Mrs Howard. "Well done, Antonia and Cai. Let's give them a round of applause."

The class clapped enthusiastically as Antonia and Cai went back to their seats. Mrs Howard flicked through the newspaper until she came to the Entertainment section.

"Here we are," she said. "There's a whole page on *Stage Struck* with a photo of the leading actors, Danny Appleton and Kate Mellor."

"And me and Becky," said Lauren, casually fluffing up her hair.

"I'm sorry, Lauren," said Mrs Howard, shaking her head. "There's not a picture of you or Becky here."

"But there must be. The photographer took loads of photos of us, didn't he Becks?"

Mrs Howard looked sympathetic. "There obviously wasn't enough room to include another photo, but you have got a mention. It says, "Lucky local girls Becky Nickson and Laura Hampton have been given parts as extras on the show.""

"Laura!" screeched Lauren. "Did you say Laura Hampton?"

"Oh dear," said Mrs Howard, scanning the article again. "They've got your name wrong. That's a shame, but it's not uncommon in a newspaper. Right then 6H, it's time to get on with some work. Maths books out, please."

Chairs scraped noisily as the class went to get their maths books from their trays. Antonia was going back to her chair with hers when

Lauren deliberately bumped against her shoulder.

"Loser!" she said nastily.

"Right now I'd say you were the loser," said Toby, who happened to be standing nearby.

Lauren narrowed her eyes. "We'll see," she hissed threateningly.

For the rest of the week Lauren kept deliberately bumping into Antonia and knocking things off her desk or her peg in the cloakroom. Antonia calmly put up with it, refusing to tell the teacher, even though Sophie and Toby both thought she should.

"Lauren shouldn't be allowed to get away with it," said Sophie hotly. "She's a bully."

"Yes," Antonia agreed. "And if she was upsetting me or hurting me then I would tell Mrs Howard. But I'm not upset and Lauren

wouldn't dare hurt me with you lot around. She's a coward at heart. Mum says that bullies usually are."

Antonia popped a crisp in her mouth and handed round the bag, smiling to cover the irritation she was feeling inside. She didn't want to think about Lauren any more.

On Friday Lauren seemed more excitable than usual and spent the day whispering with Becky. Each time Antonia came across them Lauren would make a show of falling silent. It was obvious that Lauren had a secret and wanted to make her curious, but instead Antonia found it funny. Did Lauren really think that Antonia had so little going on in her own life that she was bothered about what Lauren was up to?

At last Friday was over and the weekend

was here to enjoy. Antonia spent Saturday at Sea Watch with Cai. They were the only volunteers that day so there was lots of work to do cleaning out the gulls, Billy the razorbill and a couple of other seabirds that had been brought in with minor injuries.

It was late afternoon before Antonia went home, happily tired and still thinking about Sea Watch. She plodded up Sandy Bay Road and turned into the street that led to hers. Halfway down the street Antonia felt a familiar tingling sensation spread through her. She stood still for a moment just to be sure, but the tingling continued. Knowing what was coming next, Antonia turned round and headed quickly towards the footpath to Gull Bay. She'd almost reached it when her silver dolphin charm started vibrating, its tiny body

tapping against her neck in a steady rhythm. Halfway along the path, Antonia heard a whistling cry.

Silver Dolphin, we need you.

Spirit, I hear your call, she answered, running even faster.

Although Antonia knew the path very well, she still had to concentrate on not slipping on the loose stones. Part of her was also listening for Spirit as she burst from the path and on to the beach, pulling off her shoes the moment she hit the sand. It came as a shock to discover that she wasn't alone. Suddenly she was aware of voices. Antonia looked up and immediately went cold. A group of teenagers was having a noisy picnic on the beach. Several rugs were spread out on the sand to make one large area that was loaded with food and drink. People

sat round the edge eating from plastic plates while others danced to music from an iPod and speakers.

Silver Dolphin, we need you.

Even above the noise of the music Antonia heard Spirit's shrill whistle. Grabbing her shoes, she slunk towards the rocks. She'd often gone into the water from a crowded beach. Usually people were too busy enjoying themselves to notice her. Today would surely be no different. Antonia knew that if she could make it into the water unseen she could immediately dive out of sight and swim out of the bay underwater.

Spirit, I'm on my way.

Antonia arranged her shoes and socks behind a rock, but as she was about to go into the water a familiar voice shouted, "I knew

it! Didn't I tell you that if *she* found out about our party she'd show up?"

Antonia's stomach seemed to flip-flop as she slowly turned to face the beach again.

Lauren's face was contorted in a nasty sneer as she pointed straight at Antonia. "Go away," she said loudly. "We're having a private party for the cast of *Stage Struck* and you are not invited."

"What is she like?" asked Becky, in an equally loud voice. "She must have been snooping around at school to find out about this. And then to have the nerve to try and gatecrash... well, that's plain sad."

A few members of the cast looked up to see what the shouting was about. Antonia's face flamed and her heart hammered against her chest. She was so embarrassed. But more

importantly, how was she going to answer Spirit's call? There was no way she could go into the water now. Not if she wanted to keep her special secret.

Chapter Eleven

Spirit's whistling cry sounded again, spurring Antonia into action. If she couldn't get into the sea at Gull Bay, then she would have to go somewhere else. The next accessible beach was Sandy Bay, but it was a good fifteen minutes walk away. Antonia's heart plummeted. Scooping up her things, she headed off the beach.

"Loser," called Lauren.

"Sad, crazy girl," joined in Becky.

Antonia hardly heard them. This was madness. What if Spirit's call was a life or death situation? She needed to be in the sea right now, not turning her back on it. But knowing this wasn't an option, Antonia hurried up the steps, stopping at the top to shove her feet into her shoes and her socks in the pockets of her fleece. Antonia ran up the footpath, stopping only when her heart was thundering so loudly she thought that if she didn't rest it might explode through her chest.

Spirit, I'm on my way, she called silently, leaning against a tree for support. There was no answer. Taking a few more deep breaths, Antonia set off at a jog.

"I can do this!" she told herself as she ran along the path. "And there's Cai. If it's life or death, then Cai will already be there."

Antonia could see Sandy Bay from the Coastal Path and she gazed longingly at it. If only she could fly then she could be down there in seconds, diving into the sapphire-blue water like a gull going after a fish. On she ran until at last she was on the soft, gold beach.

Sand sprayed up from her feet as Antonia pounded towards the rocks. Then her foot caught against something and she stumbled, landing face down.

"Eew!" Pushing her hair back, Antonia spat out a mouth of sand. As she sat up something jabbed into her calf, making her flinch. She moved her leg and uncovered a sleek, black mobile phone.

"Rats!" exclaimed Antonia, picking the phone up. That was all she needed right now – an expensive piece of litter that its owner would be missing. Impulsively, Antonia stuck the phone in the pocket of her fleece meaning to sort it out later. Back on her feet again, she continued over to the rocks where she ripped off her shoes and removed her fleece. Seconds later she was in the sea, submerging her body with a running dive. Annoyingly, she was being called back towards Gull Bay. Antonia could feel her muscles straining as she arched her body in and out of the water, clearing the waves like a racehorse clearing fences.

Rounding the headland, Antonia swam east along the rocky coast between Sandy Bay and Gull Bay and sensed vibrations in the water.

They were nearer to the coast than she was, so altering her direction she swam inshore. Then Antonia saw two dolphins agitatedly swimming figures of eight. Seeing her approaching the largest dolphin broke away and came towards her.

"Silver Dolphin," clicked Spirit, clearly relieved to see her. "Go quickly, you're needed on the beach." He pointed his nose towards the rocky cliffs.

At first Antonia couldn't see where he meant, but she swam towards the rocks, trusting Spirit to send her in the right direction. The cliffs towered above and as she drew closer Antonia could see an indent in the coastline. Swimming past the rocks she arrived at a tiny cove with a small patch of sand. Cai was already there, his dark curly head bent

over a small shape. He seemed to be struggling with something. Antonia swam on, her heart hammering as fear swept over her. Dreading what she might find, she ran through the frothy surf and on to the beach.

"Tilly!" she gasped, after realising that Cai was tending to a small seal.

Hoping in vain that she was mistaken, Antonia sank to her knees.

"What happened?" she asked.

"Tilly nearly got strangled!"

Cai's fingers worked to free Tilly from a long black cable tightly wound round her neck. "She was choking when I found her. I've managed to loosen it enough to let her breathe, but I can't untie the rest of the cable. It's in too much of a knot from when she was struggling."

Antonia stroked Tilly's head, wincing at the dark red weal on her neck. "It's terrible," said Cai, his voice choked with emotion. "I thought I was going to lose her at first. What happened to you? You took ages."

"The cast of *Stage Struck* were having a party on the beach at Gull Bay when I arrived there so I had to swim from Sandy Bay instead," said Antonia, tracing her fingers frantically along the thick black cable snaking round Tilly's soft grey body, looking for a loose spot.

"What is this stuff?" Antonia wondered aloud. "It's lethal."

"Can't you guess?" asked Cai. "It's some kind of heavy-duty electrical cable. I bet it's come from the *Stage Struck* film set."

Finding a large knot Antonia worked at it

until her fingers were sore, but the cable refused to come undone. "It keeps stretching itself tighter," she complained.

Suddenly Tilly decided she'd had enough of keeping still. She began to roll from side to side, flapping her tail and one free flipper.

"Steady," said Antonia, in a soothing voice. "Tilly, steady."

At first the seal didn't seem to listen, but Antonia continued speaking in a low, calm voice while Cai gently and rhythmically stroked Tilly's head. Gradually she began to relax, resting her head back on the sand and half-closing her dark eyes.

Antonia realised she needed something sharp to cut the cable, so she jumped up and searched the sand for a stone. She found one a short way up the beach, flinty grey and

shaped like a tear drop, and ran back to Tilly and Cai. Holding the stone at its rounded end, Antonia pressed its top against the cable.

Cut.

Magic rushed along her arms, reaching her fingers in a sudden burst of warmth.

Cut, thought Antonia, enjoying the sensation as the stone sliced through the cable like a knife cutting soft butter. Carefully she attacked the knots, keeping the stone away from Tilly's fur and Cai's fingers as he pulled the cable free.

The last bit of cable fell away and as Cai gathered it up, Antonia examined the weal around Tilly's neck. It was deep in places with spots of blood breaking through the skin.

"Does it need treating?" asked Cai, putting

the looped cable over his head to wear it like a sash.

"Yes," said Antonia, taking a deep breath and preparing herself to help the seal again. Placing both hands on Tilly's soft skin, Antonia focused on making her better.

Heal.

She stared at the red area and imagined it being replaced with healthy skin and fur.

Heal.

A rush of warmth spread along Antonia's hands and into her fingers so fast that she wouldn't have been surprised if her hands had started to glow! The damaged skin began to heal, changing colour until only a faint, pink line was left. Antonia sank back on her heels, exhausted.

Tilly's whiskers twitched and she uttered a

startled honk. She lay still for a moment, thanking Antonia and Cai with her eyes, then slowly she wiggled towards the sea. As she slid into the water Antonia called out, "Bye, Tilly."

"And this time keep out of trouble!" Cai added.

Tilly was much more graceful in the water than on land. She swiftly cut through the sea until she dived under and disappeared just beyond the rocks.

"The tide's coming in," said Cai, realising his feet were getting wet.

"It's come in quickly," said Antonia.

"We'd better go," said Cai. "It must almost be high tide. This beach will be underwater soon."

"Are you all right to swim with that cable

or do you need help?" asked Antonia, pointing at the loops around his body.

"Piece of cake," said Cai, cheekily. "Come on. I'll race you back."

Chapter Twelve

s Antonia and Cai headed towards open water, four dolphins swam to meet them – Spirit, followed by Star, with Bubbles and Dream bringing up the rear.

"Well done, Silver Dolphins," said Spirit, nudging Antonia and Cai with his nose. "You did a good job."

"Can we play now, Dad?" asked Bubbles, who was impatiently bobbing in the water.

Antonia was tired after using so much strong magic, but she perked up on seeing her dolphin friends. She badly hoped that Spirit would let them play. It felt like ages since she'd last had fun with Bubbles and Dream.

"If the Silver Dolphins want to play with you," said Spirit, opening his mouth in a wide grin that showed his perfect white teeth.

"Of course they want to," said Bubbles confidently. "Who's in for sprat? I'll be it. You've got a three waves' head start."

"I'm in," clicked Antonia.

"Me too," agreed Cai and Dream.

As Bubbles started counting, Dream dived under the water. Antonia chased after her

immediately, knowing that Dream was good at finding places to hide. Cai had the same idea and they swam in a procession to a long line of rocks that looked like a sleeping crocodile. Ducking down behind the largest, Dream indicated with her flipper for Antonia and Cai to join her. Giggling softly, they squeezed together, trying to make themselves smaller.

"I've missed you," clicked Dream softly, as they waited for Bubbles to find them.

"I've missed you too," Antonia clicked back, suddenly realising how true it was. All the tension of the past weeks caused by Lauren's pettiness and nasty remarks suddenly drained away, leaving her fizzing with excitement. When Bubbles crept up behind them, clicking, "Sprat!" at the top of his voice, Antonia was

the first away. She sped upwards and leapt out of the water like a breeching whale, causing a mini tidal wave when she splash-landed again.

"Water fight!" clicked Bubbles, who'd chased her to the surface. He smacked his tail in the sea, soaking Antonia with water.

"Boys against girls," clicked Cai, breaking through the water next.

"No, every dolphin for himself," clicked Bubbles, playfully soaking Cai.

It was one of the longest water fights they'd ever had. Using tails and flippers, legs and hands, they stirred up a storm in the sea. And even when Dream finally called for a truce, Bubbles and Cai still kept flicking sea water at each other.

"That was so much fun," said Antonia,

floating on her back with her blonde hair fanned out around her.

"We're going fishing next. That's fun too. Come with us," clicked Bubbles.

Antonia sighed. "I'd love to, but I think I'd better go home. If I don't get back in time for tea, Mum and Dad will worry."

"Me too," said Cai. "Claudia will know where I am, but I don't want to miss tea. I'm starving!"

"You're always starving," said Antonia, laughing.

Bubbles swam forward as if to rub his nose against Cai's, but at the last moment he somersaulted, splashing Cai with his tail.

"Bubbles, that's enough," clicked Dream, even though she was laughing.

Bubbles grinned cheekily, then said a proper

goodbye to the Silver Dolphins. Antonia and Cai trod water as Bubbles and Dream swam out to sea, watching their silver bodies arching together in perfect time.

"Home!" said Antonia when the dolphins were specks in the distance.

They hadn't swum far when Cai said, "It may be cool having a film crew here and knowing you're going to see all your favourite places on television, but it's a nightmare too, and not just the littering. I keep worrying that we'll get seen and it'll be the end of the Silver Dolphins."

"I know," said Antonia quietly, remembering how her magic had suddenly drained away when Mr Brewer and his assistant had almost caught her being a Silver Dolphin.

They swam in silence until they approached

the Sandy Bay headland. Antonia stopped and said, "Can you hear that?"

Cai frowned and trod water to listen. "Someone's shouting," he said.

Antonia's face paled to almost the same shade as her hair and suddenly her limbs felt weak and wobbly. "Are they shouting at us?" she asked hoarsely.

Cai grabbed her hand and suddenly pulled her under the water. Antonia was so startled she swallowed a mouthful of sea.

"Yuk!" she choked, spitting it out.

"Sorry," said Cai. "But there's a man sitting far out on the rocks. He was facing the other way when I first saw him, but then he turned around towards us."

"What's he doing on the rocks?" asked Antonia. "Is he fishing?"

"If he is, he won't catch much," said Cai wryly. "Fishermen are usually very quiet so they don't scare the fish."

Antonia was horrified. "He's stuck, isn't he? I bet that's why he's shouting."

"Probably," said Cai. "He must have gone for a walk over the rocks and got cut off by the tide. He can't be a local or he'd know how fast the sea comes in round here."

"Now what?" asked Antonia. "We can't leave him there. It's too dangerous. If he slips and falls he could drown."

"But if we help him we'll blow our secret," said Cai.

"He's going to need search and rescue or something," said Antonia in a scared voice.

Cai brightened. "Perhaps that's why he's shouting. I bet he's called the emergency

services on his mobile and now he's making sure they find him when they arrive... Antonia, what's wrong? Why are you looking at me like that?"

Antonia stared at Cai, her grey-green eyes wide with concern. "But what if that man lost his phone?" she whispered. "What if he dropped it on the beach before he got caught out by the tide?"

Chapter Thirteen

Antonia told Cai about the mobile phone she'd found on the beach and he agreed that it could well belong to the man on the rocks.

"Either way, it doesn't look like he has a phone," said Cai, who'd gone to the surface to have another look. "He's shouting for help and he sounds really scared."

Antonia insisted on having a look too. Diving back underwater she said, "He looks familiar. He reminds me of... no, wait! I know who he is. It's Mr Brewer, the director." Her face contorted as she said wryly. "I know he's in serious trouble, but I can't help thinking that maybe if he hadn't been so mean about the kittiwake and his film crew's rubbish, then this wouldn't have happened."

"There's a saying for that," Cai chipped in. "What goes around comes around."

He touched the electrical cable hanging over his chest and grinned.

"You're right, it is kind of fitting. We'd better get back to Sandy Bay as fast as we can and ring the coastguard for help."

Cai was about to start swimming away underwater, but Antonia stopped him.

"You go," she said. "I'll wait here just in case he slips and falls. The tide's really high and some of those waves are enormous. I'd feel awful if Mr Brewer got swept off the rocks and drowned."

"But how are you going to help him if he falls in the sea?" asked Cai. "The moment you try and rescue him your Silver Dolphin magic will stop working, because you wouldn't be helping sea life. You're an ace swimmer, Antonia, but are you really strong enough to be swimming out here? Mr Brewer might not be the only one who ends up drowning."

Antonia fell silent, knowing that Cai was right.

"Let's get going," said Cai gently.

Antonia swam to the surface to check on

Mr Brewer before they left. He had his back pressed against the rocks, trying to keep as far away as possible from the breaking waves. His clothes were soaked and he looked small and frightened.

Antonia and Cai swam round the headland and back to Sandy Bay in silence, keeping underwater until their knees scrapped the seabed. Antonia was first out, splashing through the waves, sea water pouring from her clothes and hair as she stumbled across the rocks. She grabbed her fleece and rifled through the pockets, pulling out the mobile phone.

"How do you switch it on?" she asked, staring at the phone's smooth face.

"Here, let me." Cai calmly held out his hand, then studied the phone while Antonia hopped up and down beside him.

"It's a smart phone," he said, pressing a button at the bottom. "My dad has one. Let's just hope it doesn't have a key code like Dad's does."

A picture of the world and the time in digital figures appeared on screen, then an arrow with the words, 'slide to unlock'. Holding his breath, Cai slid his finger along the arrow. There was a sharp click and the screen's image changed to rows of coloured boxes.

"Phew! No code." Cai pressed the green box with the phone symbol, then typed 999.

Antonia bent her head closer to Cai's as she listened to the phone's shrill dialling tone. Seconds later a woman's voice answered, clear and calm. "Which emergency service do you require: fire, police or ambulance?"

"Coastguard, please," said Cai. "A man is stranded on the headland, just east of Sandy Bay."

The lady took more details, then reassured Cai that help was on its way. Cai's hands were trembling when he finished the call.

"That felt weird," he said, handing the phone back to Antonia.

Antonia squeezed his arm. "You did brilliantly," she said, perching on a rock to put on her shoes and socks.

"Here," said Cai, handing her the mobile. "You take this and I'll carry the cable."

"We'll hand the phone in at the police station. If it is Mr Brewer's, he won't have to know who found it or how. Let's do that now."

"Wait!" Antonia paused, adding quietly,

"I'd like to stay and make sure that the rescue services come. I can't get Mr Brewer's face out of my mind. He looked petrified and some of those waves were really big. I'd feel happier knowing that he's been rescued."

Cai nodded and they waited anxiously until out of the distance came the deep throb of a helicopter. Antonia jumped up, shielding her eyes to stare at the sky.

"There," she shouted, her voice catching, "a Sea King."

The roar of the incoming helicopter became deafening. Antonia stared at its massive red and grey body in awe. She'd seen the Sea King rescue helicopters flying over the bay before, but never this low. It was brilliant! The downdraft blew her hair

all over her face. Antonia swept it away
impatiently, her eyes never leaving the
helicopter as it banked and flew along the
coastline. The enormous side door was open
and two figures dressed in overalls hung
out, staring at the rocks. Antonia swallowed
and rubbed away tears with the back of her
hand.

"Woohoo!" yelled Cai, his face shiny with
excitement as a man with a safety harness
was lowered on to the rocks beside Mr Brewer
and waved back at the helicopter.

Antonia burst out laughing. "We did it!" she
yelled back. "Mr Brewer's going to be fine."

"It's not fair," grumbled Cai, as they made
their way off the beach. "I'd love a ride in a
helicopter. Why can't I get stranded on the
rocks?"

"Because you wouldn't be my friend if you were that stupid!" said Antonia helpfully. "Besides," she continued, "we go swimming with dolphins. It doesn't get better than that."

Chapter Fourteen

Antonia wasn't looking forward to Monday. She knew Lauren would taunt her about accidentally turning up at the *Stage Struck* beach party. Leaving the house much later than usual, Antonia walked slowly round to Sophie's. Her friend had tired of waiting for her and met Antonia at the corner of her road.

"Lazy legs!" Sophie scolded. "What took you so long? I thought you weren't coming. Have you heard about the director of *Stage Struck*?"

"Yes," said Antonia. "You couldn't miss it."

Mr Brewer's rescue had made it on to the local news and the Sandy Bay radio station.

"He's recovering in hospital so they'll probably have to stop filming, won't they," Sophie said glumly.

"I don't know," said Antonia. "What about the assistant director? Wouldn't she be able to take over? I don't think they'd just pack up and go home. It'd be too expensive to come back again."

Sophie perked up. "I hope you're right! I've just got friendly with one of the girls who works on the scenery. She promised to show me all the props they'd brought with them

and the paints they use to touch things up."

"Why don't you ask Lauren or Becky? I expect they'll know what's happening," Antonia suggested.

"No way!" Sophie was outraged. "In case you haven't noticed, I only speak to Lauren when I have to. You're my best friend, Antonia. If Lauren's mean to you, then I'm not going to be chatty with her."

"Thanks," said Antonia, knowing she was lucky to have a friend as loyal as Sophie.

School wasn't as bad as Antonia had expected. Lauren was too busy answering questions about the director's dramatic rescue to remember Antonia being at the beach party. A large crowd of children gathered round her and Becky in the playground, and Lauren's face was positively glowing with the attention.

"Well, Danny said to me, yes, Danny Appleton who plays Josh… yeah, course we're mates. I've got his mobile number and everything…"

But it wasn't until after lunch when Antonia overheard Lauren reminding Mrs Howard that she needed to leave early as the assistant director was starting filming at 3pm, that Antonia had her brilliant idea. She was out of her seat in a flash to share it with Cai, but Mrs Howard made her sit down again.

"Story writing this afternoon, timed and in silence," announced Mrs Howard, ignoring the groans. "I want an adventure story, but nothing too gory and no rescue stories about people getting trapped on the rocks by a high tide. I've heard quite enough tales about that for one day."

Antonia liked writing stories, but found it impossible to concentrate. Her brain felt frozen and she spent ages agonising over what to write. At 2.45pm Lauren and Becky made a big show of leaving early. Mrs Howard growled at them as they handed in their work.

"Sssh! Or you won't be going anywhere, even if your parents have both written me notes to excuse you early."

When the bell went, Antonia couldn't get out of the classroom fast enough.

"What did Claudia do with the cable that we found wrapped round Tilly?" she asked Cai.

Cai stared at her as if she was mad. "She put it in the bin I think. Why, do you want it?"

"Yes," said Antonia, pulling him along the

corridor and out of the school building. "Hurry, I've had an idea."

When they arrived at Sea Watch, Antonia put her idea to Claudia too. "Louise, the assistant director, is in charge today. She was much nicer than Mr Brewer when they caught me trying to rescue the kittiwake. Let's take the cable back to her and explain how dangerous litter is to sea life. She might be more helpful than Mr Brewer was."

"We'll go and see her now," said Claudia decisively. "The cable's in the dustbin. Put on some gloves to get it out, then drop it in the back of my car. I'll just shut the computer down and tell Sally that we're going out."

Antonia and Cai sat in the back of the car with the cable on the floor between them.

Antonia spent the whole journey nervously twiddling a strand of her hair.

"Is everything all right?" asked Claudia, catching her eye in the rear-view mirror.

"Fine, thanks," said Antonia brightly, even though she was incredibly nervous.

What if Louise refused to help? Worse still, what if she'd misjudged Louise and she called them names like Mr Brewer had? Antonia closed her eyes, not even wanting to think about what Lauren would say the following day at school.

The ride to Gull Bay was over far too quickly. Claudia parked her car behind the film crew's blue transit van and they walked along the last part of the footpath to the beach. Antonia's stomach fizzed and popped like a sparkler on bonfire night, but she held her head high as she followed Claudia through a crowd of people towards the camera crew.

"I'm looking for the assistant director, please," Claudia politely asked a young man holding a sound boom.

"She's over there," said the man, jerking his head towards a small group of people.

Antonia's heart plummeted right down to her toes. She recognised Louise at once, looking smart and very in control as she briefed a group of actors, including Lauren.

Lauren's eyes narrowed when she saw Antonia.

Antonia deliberately looked away. What did it matter if Lauren called her names? Louise was the important person. For the sake of the dolphins, for Tilly and for all the other sea

life, they needed put a stop to the rubbish being created by *Stage Struck*.

"Can I help you?" asked Louise pleasantly.

"I hope so. I'm Claudia Neale, from a marine conservation charity called Sea Watch. I'm here to talk to you about litter," Claudia said, smiling at Louise.

At the back of the group Lauren yawned loudly. "Not that again!" she grumbled.

Louise looked up in surprise. "Sorry, Laura, isn't it? Did you have something to say?"

Blushing furiously, Lauren shook her head. Antonia hid a smile. Poor Lauren. Antonia decided it would make her feel very unhappy to be as mean as Lauren was the whole time.

Louise listened carefully to Claudia, nodding as she spoke. When Claudia had finished, Louise shook her hand. "Thank you for coming

to see us again. I'm sorry you weren't taken seriously last time. Dropping litter is inexcusable. It's been worrying me ever since I saw that bird suffering on the cliff ledge. Now that I'm in charge, I'll make sure that our rubbish is cleared at the end of each day." Taking the cable from Claudia she added, "This was plain carelessness. Apart from the injuries that this lost equipment could cause, there's also the matter of expense. We don't have an unlimited budget. Thanks again for bringing it to my attention."

Louise and Claudia shook hands warmly. Antonia grinned at Cai, silently giving him the thumbs up. This was better than she'd hoped for. Louise had not only promised to be more careful, but was also going to personally supervise a clear-up every day.

Subconsciously, Antonia reached for the silver dolphin charm tucked inside her polo shirt. Her fingers brushed its soft body and were rewarded with a flick of the dolphin's tail. Antonia stared out to sea. Was it a trick of the light or could she see four silver shapes flashing across the mouth of the bay?

She was about to nudge Cai when the shapes dived underwater.

Spirit, thought Antonia with a smile.

Silver Dolphin, he replied.

Silver Dolphins

OUT
NOW!

Silver Dolphins join forces with local fishermen to save a
whale from being stranded in the river, but it keeps
returning. And is this the end of Silver Dolphins for Cai?

HarperCollins *Children's Books*

Buy more great Silver Dolphins books from HarperCollins at 10% off recommended retail price. FREE postage and packing in the UK.

Out Now:

Silver Dolphins – The Magic Charm	ISBN: 978-0-00-730968-9
Silver Dolphins – Secret Friends	ISBN: 978-0-00-730969-6
Silver Dolphins – Stolen Treasures	ISBN: 978-0-00-730970-2
Silver Dolphins – Double Danger	ISBN: 978-0-00-730971-9
Silver Dolphins – Broken Promises	ISBN: 978-0-00-730972-6
Silver Dolphins – Moonlight Magic	ISBN: 978-0-00-730973-3
Silver Dolphins – Rising Star	ISBN: 978-0-00-734812-1
Silver Dolphins – Stormy Skies	ISBN: 978-0-00-734813-8
Silver Dolphins – High Tide	ISBN: 978-0-00-736749-8
Silver Dolphins – River Rescue	ISBN: 978-0-00-736750-4

All priced at £4.99

To purchase by Visa/Mastercard/Switch simply call
08707871724 or fax on **08707871725**

To pay by cheque, send a copy of this form with a cheque made payable to 'HarperCollins Publishers' to: Mail Order Dept. (Ref: BOB4), HarperCollins Publishers, Westerhill Road, Bishopbriggs, G64 2QT, making sure to include your full name, postal address and phone number.

From time to time HarperCollins may wish to use your personal data to send you details of other HarperCollins publications and offers. If you wish to receive information on other HarperCollins publications and offers please tick this box ☐

Do not send cash or currency. Prices correct at time of press.
Prices and availability are subject to change without notice.
Delivery overseas and to Ireland incurs a £2 per book postage and packing charge.